Rodgers and Hammerstein's

 For information address Disney Press, 114 Fifth Avenue, New York, New York 10011-5690.

Printed in the United States.

First Edition
1 3 5 7 9 10 8 6 4 2

This book is set in 12-point Palatino.

Library of Congress Catalog Card Number: 97-80132

ISBN: 0-7868-4209-1

Rodgers and Hammerstein's

Teleplay by Robert L. Freedman
Adapted by Rita Walsh Balducci
Based on the original television musical *Cinderella*
Music by Richard Rodgers
Book and Lyrics by Oscar Hammerstein II

114 Fifth Avenue
New York, NY 10011-5690

Chapter 1

"Move it!"

Cinderella looked up, startled from her daydreams. Her cruel stepsister Calliope was shoving a heavy package into her already overloaded arms.

"Hurry up!" urged Minerva, her other stepsister. "Stop your daydreaming!"

Cinderella sighed. Far-fetched though they were, daydreams were the only source of joy in her life. "Coming!" she said, picking up her pace.

The young women followed a haughty older woman through the crowded streets of the village, stopping when she stopped. She was Calliope's and Minerva's mother—Cinderella's stepmother.

"Oh, look!" cried Minerva, reaching for a plumed hat outside the hatmaker's shop. She plopped it onto her head and peered at her

reflection in the shop window. "What do you think, Mother?"

"I saw it first!" pouted Calliope.

Their mother frowned. "It's a little . . . well, it's rather . . . what do you think, Cinderella?"

Cinderella gulped as the three women looked at her expectantly. She shrugged and did her best to be honest.

"I . . . I don't know much about hats," she replied, "but I don't think it flatters either one of you. . . ."

The stepsisters gasped.

"Doesn't flatter us?" cried Minerva. "What do you know?"

"She said she doesn't know anything about hats," Calliope said. "She's just jealous!"

Cinderella said nothing as the sisters turned their attention back to the hideous hat.

"Let me try it on!" whined Calliope. "Your head's too big for it!"

Minerva held the hat high out of Calliope's reach. "Mother!" she cried.

The sisters followed their mother into the shop, their loud voices carrying out into the street. Cinderella shook her head as she listened to them fight.

It was a busy morning, and Cinderella

watched as the townspeople hurried about their errands. In her mind, though, she was far away with her one true love.

"He's out there . . . somewhere!" she whispered to herself. "My love is waiting for me . . . whoever he is!"

"CINDERELLA!"

Cinderella jumped. There were Calliope, Minerva, and her stepmother, piling even more bundles into her arms.

"Have you ever seen a lazier girl in your whole life?" Minerva remarked.

Cinderella tightened her grip on the boxes and bags and trailed behind them. Her dreams would have to wait.

Not far from town, an ornate carriage slowed to a stop. The door opened, and out jumped a handsome young man wearing a jeweled crown.

"Your highness, *please* . . . ," began Lionel, his footman. "This can't go on!"

The prince tossed his crown to Lionel. Then he ran his hands through his hair and stretched.

"Oh, Lionel! It feels good to be free of the crown, even if just for a little while!" the prince said as he pulled off his heavy gloves.

Lionel shook his head in frustration. "But going about town disguised as a common

peasant!" he moaned. "What would the king and queen say?"

The prince laughed at the thought. "They won't say anything . . . because you won't tell them! I'll meet you back at the palace!" And with that, he was off.

"You were expected back an hour ago!" Lionel called pleadingly. "Your highness!" He sighed and climbed back into the carriage.

The prince bounded into town, anxious to experience as much village life as possible before he had to return to the formality of the palace. His face lit up at the sights, sounds, and smells of the busy marketplace. Vendors cried out, children played, villagers shopped for bargains—and not one of them knew he was the prince. There was so much to do! So much to see!

"Watch where you're going, you nincompoop!"

The prince spun around, coming face to face with Cinderella's cruel stepmother and clumsy sisters. "I beg your pardon," he said with a low bow.

The stepmother and her daughters sneered. "Fool!" they snorted as they barged past.

Cinderella struggled to keep up. The pile of packages made it difficult for her to see where she was going. Without realizing it, she was walking right into the path of the royal carriage!

"Look out!" cried the prince, catching Cinderella in his arms. He pulled her out of harm's way into a nearby alley.

"Are you all right, Miss?" he asked, helping to gather the fallen packages.

"I . . . I'm fine, I think," Cinderella stammered, trying to catch her breath.

The prince knelt beside her. "Here, let me help you," he said, his voice full of concern. "What's your name?"

Cinderella looked up warily. She was not used to people showing much interest in her. "Cinderella," she said softly.

"Excuse me?" the prince said in confusion.

"Cinderella. I like to sit next to the fire, but the cinders smudge my face when I get too close. So my nickname became Cinderella. I've given up trying to stop people from calling me that. It just stuck. Now it's the only name anyone ever calls me."

"I like it," the prince said with a smile. "It's different. Like you."

Their eyes met. Cinderella felt her heart pound a little faster. She looked away quickly.

"Um, I better go," she said nervously.

"What's your hurry?" asked the prince, blocking her path.

Cinderella tried to pass him, but he ducked in front of her again, a broad smile on his face.

"Tell me, what does a man have to do to find himself in your good graces?" he asked.

A dreamy look came over Cinderella's face. "First," she said quietly, "he'd have to treat me right."

"Like a princess, I suppose," the prince mused.

"Like a *person*," Cinderella corrected him. Then her voice got wistful as she went on. "I want kindness, and respect."

"Everyone gets that," the prince said matter-of-factly.

Cinderella stared at him. "You just don't get it, do you?" she said.

The prince hurried to explain. "Please don't take offense," he said. "It's just that . . . I've lived a kind of sheltered existence."

Their eyes met again, but this time Cinderella looked steadily into the prince's eyes. "I know what you mean," she whispered, and then said, "Have you ever felt like running away somewhere and never coming back?"

Before the prince could reply, the magical

moment was spoiled by the shrill voice of Cinderella's stepmother calling for her.

"What is the meaning of this?" shrieked the stepmother. "I thought I told you never to talk to strangers!"

The prince backed away, shocked by the woman's rage. Cinderella hung her head in humiliation.

"I hope to see you again . . . Cinderella," called the prince gently.

Cinderella turned from her stepmother to watch him disappear into the crowded marketplace.

"Good-bye," she said under her breath.

"CINDERELLA!" shrieked her stepmother.

And with that, she gathered her packages and started for home.

chapter 2

That evening, the prince was summoned to his parents' quarters. "I hope they haven't found out about my trips to the village," he muttered, "or Lionel will have a lot of explaining to do!"

With a deep breath and a careful smile, he entered the queen's boudoir.

"You wanted to see me, Mother?" he asked.

The queen rose from her place, taking his arm. "Darling!" she cried happily. "Your father and I have been talking about you. . . ."

"Keep me out of this," said the king gruffly.

The prince glanced from the king to the queen anxiously. "What's going on?" he asked with a sense of dread.

The queen laughed. "Pay no attention to him! It's just that it's almost your birthday . . ."

"Oh no," said the prince.

"And I thought it ought to be celebrated . . ."

"Oh, no, no, no," groaned the prince.

"With a small gathering of friends . . . ," the queen went on.

"Mother, please," begged the prince.

"And of course, all the eligible women in the kingdom," the queen finished.

"WHAT?!" cried the prince, collapsing into a chair.

"Four or five hundred at the most," the queen said, patting his hand soothingly.

"Mother, listen to me," the prince said determinedly. "I do not want a ball!"

But the queen paid no attention. "My dear boy, of course you do!"

"He doesn't want a ball," repeated the king.

With that, the queen gasped. Her hand flew to her forehead dramatically. The prince rolled his eyes.

"Now, Mother," he said sternly. "You must not do this!"

The queen sat up. "But darling! You must think about getting married! It's your obligation as prince!"

The prince nodded sympathetically. "I know, Mother. But please. I must find a wife for myself. I want to fall in love. I want to be happy."

"But darling, what does *happy* have to do with it?" the queen asked innocently.

The prince threw up his hands and stormed out of the room.

The king and queen watched him go, astonished by his reaction.

"We'll have the ball," the king reassured his wife.

"The prince will thank us for it later. I'm sure of it," she cooed. "Now let's start planning!"

By the next day, the whole town was buzzing with the news of the prince's birthday ball. Lionel had been assigned the task of spreading the word, and the villagers were surprised and delighted.

"The prince is giving a ball!" he sang high and low. "The prince is giving a ball!"

Calliope and Minerva were soon caught up in the excitement of the day. Each was convinced that the prince would fall in love with her.

"We shall need new gowns," they cried to their mother.

"Cinderella!" called the stepmother, her voice crackling with excitement. "You have your work cut out for you! We'll need these gowns made up at once! Hurry now! No dawdling!"

The stepmother heaped fabric in Cinderella's

arms and bustled after her daughters singing the song that was echoing throughout the village: "The prince is giving a ball!"

Only Cinderella had a heavy heart. "I wish I could go, too," she said with a sigh.

Chapter 3

The prince's birthday ball was the talk of the household. Gowns, gloves, hairstyles, slippers, capes, and jewelry were all Minerva, Calliope, and their mother could talk about. Cinderella listened hungrily to every detail, imagining that she too were going to the ball.

"Calliope! You're slouching!" the stepmother said. "The future queen must NOT slouch!"

"Future . . . queen?" Calliope said, straightening her back.

"Of course," the stepmother replied. "The prince will choose his wife from the eligible young ladies at the ball."

"And I'm so eligible!" giggled Minerva.

"Minerva! Lengthen your neck!" the stepmother commanded. "And after tea, we must practice our waltzing. Where *is* our tea? Cinderella!"

Cinderella jumped from her sewing. "I was just getting it, Stepmother," she said quickly.

"And another thing," the stepmother said, "have you cleaned the chimney?"

"The chimney?" Cinderella said softly. "Not yet, Stepmother. You see, I've had so much to do, with the ball tomorrow night. . . ."

"You've had too much to do?" the stepmother repeated in a mocking tone. "You ungrateful thing! Here I am, a poor widow alone in the world, trying to make the lives of my dear children just a tiny bit better, and you, you spoiled wretch, you can't even help by doing the simplest task. . . ."

"I'm sorry, Stepmother," Cinderella said. But her stepmother went on.

"You would be out in the cold if not for my big heart, Cinderella," the stepmother said icily. "Always remember that. Now bring us our tea."

Cinderella turned to go, and then turned back.

"Stepmother," she said. "I was wondering about the ball. The proclamation said that all eligible woman are to attend."

Her stepmother stared as Cinderella continued.

"If I could just have a scrap of material, I would make my own gown. It wouldn't cost much. And I would so love to go to the ball!"

"Oh, would you?" laughed the stepmother. "And why not dance with the prince while you're at it?"

Cinderella stood fast, not saying anything. At last her stepmother stopped laughing and her face became grim again.

"Know your place, my girl," she said threateningly. "The prince cannot waste his time with lowly servant girls with ashes on their faces."

"I wouldn't be a servant with ashes on my face if my father was still alive," Cinderella shot back, startled by the anger in her reply.

Her stepmother's eyebrows arched. "But he's not alive, is he? And you will do as I say."

Cinderella's hands were clenched in tight fists of rage. Her stepmother had treated her cruelly before, but this was the worst ever. Unwilling to let her stepmother see her cry, she ran into the kitchen.

Four tiny white mice scampered inside their cage as Cinderella entered the room. These were her pets, the only friends she had. Sadly, she stroked them with her fingertip and imagined a life beyond the drudgery of the kitchen and the harsh words of her stepmother.

"I know I'm only Cinderella," she said to the mice, "sitting by the fire with my daydreams. But in my dreams I'm so much more! And now, all I can dream about is going to the ball." Only the mice saw Cinderella's tears as she prepared tea that afternoon.

As the rest of the kingdom was in a frenzy of excitement about the ball, the one person it was to honor was doing his best to call it off.

"I won't have it!" the prince insisted. "You must call it off at once!"

The queen brushed his protests aside. "Nonsense, my dear," she said with a laugh. "Will there be enough wine, Lionel?"

Lionel and the prince exchanged looks. "There will be more than enough, Your Majesty," he replied.

"Mother!" the prince cried. "Are you listening to me?"

The queen looked wounded. "Of course I am, darling!" she said, her voice full of concern. "Now tell me, the red uniforms tonight, or the blue?"

The prince folded his arms across his chest and stuck out his chin. "I am not going to the ball!"

The king and queen looked shocked. "But you must!" they cried.

Lionel rolled his eyes. He had been with the royal family for many years and had witnessed many displays of stubborness before. "Ahem," he said.

All eyes turned to him expectantly.

"If I may," he said with a bow. "Perhaps a compromise can be reached. The prince will attend the ball . . ."

"Never!" the prince declared. Lionel ignored him.

". . . if Your Majesties will agree to something that His Highness wants."

The royal family considered this. Suddenly, the prince smiled. "I'll go to the ball," he said.

The queen clapped her hands giddily. "I knew you'd come around!"

The prince smiled at her. "On one condition. If I don't meet my bride tomorrow night, I will set sail the following morning."

"Set sail? But where will you go?" asked the king.

"Wherever the wind takes me," the prince answered. "I just want to get away . . . from all this!" And with a sweep of his arm toward the elaborate ballroom, he left.

Chapter 4

The day of the ball had come at last. Shopkeepers closed up early, the streets were deserted, and the air was filled with excitement as the sun began to set.

Cinderella's heart was heavy as she helped Calliope and Minerva dress, but neither stepsister noticed her forlorn face.

"I hope you haven't wrinkled my gown," Calliope cried, tugging the heavy dress from Cinderella's arms.

"Have you stretched my dancing shoes enough?" Minerva demanded. "They feel tight!"

Cinderella was so busy, she scarcely had time to remember that out of all the young women in the kingdom, she alone would be staying at home tonight.

Even the cruel stepmother was caught up in the hustle and bustle of the preparations.

"My girls will be the envy of everyone at the ball!"

"Oh, Mother, do you really think so?" Minerva cried giddily.

"Our family is known for its fascinating women," her mother answered. "Why, if I had only had the opportunities that you girls have had, I might have married a prince myself." Her face grew dark, and it twisted into its usual grimace. "My mother never pushed for me to have the things that you girls have. All she cared about was herself! She didn't sacrifice, she never lavished the gentle affections that I give you so boundlessly. . . . CALLIOPE! Sit up straight!"

The stepmother shook her head in disgust and took a deep breath to compose herself once again. Then, in as sweet a voice as she could muster, she turned to Minerva and Calliope and said, "Above all, girls, tonight you must dazzle the prince—dazzle him so he doesn't see your flaws. At least not until after the wedding! Now then, Calliope, how will you win over His Royal Highness?"

Calliope smirked at her sister, pleased to go first. "I'm going to laugh at all his jokes," she said as she demonstrated with a ladylike giggle but finished with a most unbecoming snort.

Her mother glared at her. "I do hope you will

get that snort under control before the ball!" she said. "Now, Minerva . . ."

Minerva was nervously scratching her knees.

"Minerva! Stop that scratching at once!" her mother cried.

"I can't help it!" Minerva whined. "You know how itchy I get when I'm nervous!"

"There's nothing to be nervous about," her mother said. "Now flutter your eyelashes and stop that scratching! The prince will think you have fleas!"

Minerva clasped her hands together tightly to prevent herself from scratching. "Well, Mother, I thought I'd impress the prince with a poem. . . ."

The stepmother considered this. "Very well," she said. "But beware of letting the prince know just how clever you are. Men can't bear to be around smart women, you know."

Cinderella gasped at this. Her stepmother and stepsister whirled around to face her.

"That can't be true!" Cinderella said. "Shouldn't a man love you just for who you are? Whether you're smart or pretty or plain or . . . or . . ."

"Or wearing rags?" finished the stepmother sarcastically. "And how would *you* win the prince's heart, Cinderella?"

"Well, if he were the man I wanted to marry, I'd want to know that he loved me and cared about me. And I'd have to be sure that I loved him so much that I wanted to spend the rest of my life with him. And since I couldn't spend the rest of my life pretending to be someone I'm not, it shouldn't matter if I'm smart or charming or beautiful. The important thing would be that we love each other . . . for the rest of our lives," Cinderella closed her eyes as she finished.

Minerva and Calliope swooned. "I'm going to do that!" declared Minerva.

"Me too!" sighed Calliope.

A stamp of the stepmother's foot brought them out of their daydreams. "Have you girls learned nothing from me?" she shouted. "You put that fluff out of your heads immediately! Now get moving!"

The sisters bolted for their rooms, shouting orders at Cinderella. Cinderella shook her head as she went about getting their things ready for the ball.

"Cinderella! Where's my fan?"

"Cinderella! I've lost a glove!"

"Cinderella! Call for our carriage!"

"Cinderella! Cinderella! Cinderella!"

In a flurry of capes and last-minute instructions, the stepmother and her daughters were finally on their way.

Cinderella stood in the moonlight watching the carriage join the procession of others all going in the same direction. In the distance she could see the bright lights of the palace and could almost hear the music. She tried vainly to blink back her tears until she finally rushed back into the house, slamming the door behind her.

Chapter 5

After all the evening's activity, the quiet of the house was more than Cinderella could bear. She sat down beside the fire and began to sob.

"Oh, I wish . . . I wish . . . I wish I could go to the ball!" she wept, her face buried in her arms.

A light flashed in the room. It shimmered and cast sparkles all about. Cinderella raised her head and blinked in astonishment. Suddenly, she saw a face in the window. There was a beautiful woman smiling at her!

"Who are you?" Cinderella asked, forgetting her misery.

"I'm your fairy godmother, honey," answered the woman as she entered the cellar.

Cinderella's jaw dropped. "My what?" she gasped.

The fairy godmother sighed. "I can see this

is going to take some explaining," she said. She raised her arm and pointed her wand to the window. It slammed shut. Then she pointed the wand at the pathetic little fire, and it roared into a cheerful blaze.

"That's better," the godmother said briskly.

"I guess you really are my fairy godmother!" Cinderella said in awe. Then, in a voice that was almost a whisper, she added, "I've always dreamed about someone coming to get me out of here."

Her godmother shook her head. "Dreams aren't going to work here, Cinderella. And I'm not going to get you out of here, either."

Cinderella looked crushed. "You're not?" she asked, a lump forming in her throat once again.

"No. Not me. YOU! You're the one who's going to walk out that door. There comes a time when dreamers have to become doers, Cinderella," the fairy said firmly. "And I've been watching you. I see how they treat you here. It's time."

Cinderella nodded. Her fairy godmother was right. But the thought of leaving the only home she knew, no matter how awful, was frightening. "If you only knew how many times I've wished for one of those pumpkins to turn into a coach

and take me away," she said with a little laugh. "But it's impossible."

Her godmother smiled gently. "Impossible things happen every day. You *can* go to the ball."

Cinderella looked up. Go to the ball? "Impossible things happen every day," she repeated. Her fairy godmother nodded encouragingly.

"Suppose I decided to give you a little help. But just a little! You've got to know that once you're at the ball, you're on your own," she said at last.

Cinderella gasped. "Oh, would you, Fairy Godmother? Would you really help me?" she cried in disbelief.

"Stand back!" the fairy godmother ordered. Then she stretched out her arms. Cinderella held her breath.

Nothing happened.

The fairy godmother shrugged. "You'd think after six hundred years . . . all right, I've got it now . . . I think. Here we go!"

A round yellow pumpkin, which was growing by the cellar door, began to swell and shake. Strange beams of light burst from its top, and Cinderella had to jump aside as it grew larger and larger before her very eyes. Its vines twisted into wheels, and in an instant it was transformed into the most elegant coach that Cinderella had ever seen!

The fairy godmother smiled smugly and turned her attention to the pet mice. The frightened creatures scampered about, but in a twinkle of fairy dust they became four majestic stallions.

"Oh, my!" Cinderella breathed. She reached a tentative hand up to stroke a silvery mane. "It's really happening!"

"Honey, I'm just warming up!" said the fairy godmother. "Here we go again!" And with a sweep of her arms, three scruffy rats who had come to steal corn were transformed into a coachman and two footmen in splendid uniforms.

Cinderella clapped her hands joyfully. "Oh, they're perfect! It's all so beautifully perfect! Just like in my dreams!"

Her fairy godmother eyed Cinderella critically. "Not quite perfect," she declared. "We've got to do something about that dress."

Cinderella looked down at her tattered frock and her dirty bare feet. She had almost forgotten what she looked like.

The fairy godmother squinted and furrowed her brow. "Turn around, honey," she told Cinderella. "Let's try . . . this!"

In a puff of sparkling fairy dust, Cinderella's ragged housedress and apron were replaced with a long, elegant gown of shimmering satin. Her hair was piled high on her head in a mass of glossy curls, and on her feet shone the daintiest crystal dancing shoes ever.

"Glass dancing slippers!" Cinderella cried as she held out her foot to show one off.

Her fairy godmother grinned. "I guess I just got carried away with myself," she said. "Now, there's just one more thing. . . ."

"Don't worry, I'll be very careful not to break them," Cinderella assured her.

"Break them? Oh, no, no. Not that. You've got to leave the ball by the stroke of midnight. That's when the spell ends. Sorry, but that's all the time you've got," the fairy godmother said.

Cinderella nodded, tears of joy filling her eyes. "It's more time than I ever dared to dream I'd have at the ball. Oh, thank you, Fairy Godmother! Thank you so much! This is all a dream come true!"

Cinderella's fairy godmother held up her hand. "I'm just helping you along, child. Making the dream come true is up to you. But I know you can do it. Now, you better get moving."

The footman held open the door of the coach and Cinderella stepped into its velvet interior. She leaned out the window as the four horses began to race in the direction of the castle.

"It's possible!" she cried delightedly as the coach picked up speed. Soon they were on the outskirts of town, and the glowing castle rose before them on the dark horizon.

A glittering splash of fireworks lit up the sky as Cinderella's magical carriage approached. She held her breath. Her dream was about to come true at last!

Chapter 6

The prince was having a difficult time living up to his end of the bargain. Eligible maiden after eligible maiden had been introduced to him; he danced with each one; and then she was led away. His back was sore from bowing, his face was stiff from smiling, and his feet hurt from dancing. The ladies were young and old, charming and dull, beautiful and plain, but there was none among them who struck his fancy.

"Still," he reminded himself, "a deal is a deal. Tomorrow I shall be off—away from all this nonsense once and for all!" And so he composed himself and greeted another eager young maiden.

The king and queen were more optimistic.

"So many lovely young ladies," the queen murmured. "He'll find what he's looking for tonight. There's magic in the air!"

While her stepsisters prepare for the ball, poor Cinderella scrambles to finish her housework.

"Impossible things are happening every day," Cinderella's fairy godmother says, with a twinkle in her eye.

With a touch of magic,
Cinderella's tattered dress
transforms into . . .

. . . a gorgeous gown, just
in time for the royal ball.

The wicked stepsisters' attempt to keep Cinderella from the ball doesn't work out too well, and she makes a grand entrance.

Cinderella's wicked stepsisters and stepmother are determined to be the belles of the ball, but they may have some unexpected competition!

The prince's meddling parents are curious to know who their son's beautiful new dance partner is.

Cinderella's evil stepsisters are shocked to discover Cinderella's foot fits perfectly into the glass slipper.

With the exception of two very unhappy stepsisters, the whole village gathers to celebrate Cinderella's marriage to the prince.

The king rolled his eyes. "And what if he doesn't meet the girl of his dreams? He'll be gone tomorrow, and who knows if he'll ever produce an heir to the throne."

The queen flashed her husband an incredulous look. "But my dear, he may not leave until he finds a bride. And as far as I'm concerned, this ball is not going to end until he does."

Lionel, who was standing nearby, groaned at the thought.

"My good man," a woman said impatiently, tapping him with her fan, "when will the prince be free to dance with *my* daughters?"

Lionel looked past Cinderella's stepmother to Calliope and Minerva, who stood awkwardly behind her. He began to feel sorry for the prince.

"Madam," he said haughtily, "His Highness will dance with all the young ladies in due time. Do try to exercise some restraint, I beg you."

The stepmother was taken aback, but only for a moment. She decided to try a different approach.

"Of course," the stepmother purred. "But what I want to know is, who is going to dance with *you*?"

At this, Lionel sneezed. The stepmother

continued, "Haven't you noticed something in the air between us?"

Lionel sneezed again, then blew his nose loudly. "Something in the air?" he repeated. "Madam, I believe it's your cologne."

In a violent fit of sneezing, he quickly made his retreat.

The stepmother looked up just in time to see Calliope being introduced to the prince.

"This is it!" she sang to herself. Quickly she crossed the room.

The prince held out his arm, and Calliope immediately grabbed it like a drowning person grasping a rope. As they stepped out on the dance floor, the prince signalled to the orchestra to make the song a short one.

"Oh, Your Highness! You are the funniest man! *HONK! HONK! HONK!*" Calliope began to laugh, causing everyone around them to stop dancing and stare in horror.

"Très amusant!" she laughed, trying to control the snorting but failing miserably.

Lionel finally took pity on the prince. He strode across the floor and took Calliope's arm.

"Time's up, miss," he said firmly as he led Calliope away. The prince closed his eyes and said a heartfelt thank-you to his loyal footman.

When the prince opened his eyes, he saw Minerva extending her hand to him. He quickly closed them again, praying for the night to end.

But as he opened his eyes again, Minerva was still standing there. The prince had no choice but to dance with her as quickly as he could and just get it over with.

Minerva was so nervous that she almost forgot her poem. A sharp look from her mother made her remember that this was her big chance.

"Ships that pass in the night, and speak to each other in passing . . . ," she blurted out, rather loudly.

"Excuse me?" said the prince in confusion.

"It's poetry," Minerva said. She winced. "Now I forgot where I was," she whined. "I have to start over."

The prince went pale at the thought. The young woman was beginning to scratch herself frantically as she barked out the lines of the poem she had rehearsed.

"Ships that pass in the night—that's you and me, get it?" Minerva said desperately.

"Got it," the prince replied. The song had ended at last. With a courtly nod, he turned and looked for Lionel.

"What have you gotten me into?" he hissed. "This is torture!"

Lionel patted his shoulder gently. "There, there. Only two, maybe three hundred young women left to meet. I should have such problems!"

The prince glared at him. "Tell that orchestra to speed it up! I have a ship to sail tomorrow!"

Lionel did as he was asked. The orchestra began to play at a frenzied pace.

The hot, crowded ballroom was a dizzying sight. Music was blasting and dancers were twirling in their finery as the prince mechanically danced with one young lady after another. No one seemed to be having a very good time.

"I think it's going rather well, wouldn't you agree, my dear?" the king asked his wife sarcastically.

The queen's response was a smack with her fan.

Chapter 7

Cinderella's carriage pulled up in front of the castle at last. The music from the ballroom drifted through the open windows. Her heart began to beat faster. She couldn't believe she was actually here!

The fairy godmother leaned out of the coach's window and glanced at the clock tower. It was eleven o'clock.

"All right, sugar," she said warmly. "This is where I leave you. Remember, you have to leave by midnight. You've only got an hour, but honey, I know that's all the time you'll need."

Cinderella was so excited she was shaking. She barely heard what her fairy godmother was saying. She wanted to dance all night!

When Cinderella turned back to the carriage, her fairy godmother had disappeared. Bravely,

she set one tiny, glistening foot out of the carriage and onto the marble steps of the palace.

"It's possible," she whispered to herself as she went up. "It's possible. It's possible!"

As she approached the ballroom, Cinderella heard the music get louder and louder until it was almost deafening. She stopped at the top of the stairs to catch her breath, amazed at the sight before here.

The prince was the first to see her. He stopped in his tracks, enraptured by the stunning young woman before him. Like a man in a trance, he began to walk toward her.

Soon, everyone else saw who the prince saw, and they, too, stopped what they were doing. Even the orchestra stopped the wild music. Silence filled the enormous ballroom as Cinderella gingerly descended the stairs.

Cinderella and the prince met at the bottom of the stairs, and for a moment their eyes met.

"Hello," the prince said, his voice a whisper.

"How do you do, Your Highness," Cinderella said in awe as she realized that the prince was the stranger she had spoken to in the village.

The prince offered his arm and guided Cinderella to the dance floor. She trembled as the music began. All eyes were on her, but she and the prince only had eyes for each other.

"Who is she?" buzzed the guests to one another. Everyone jostled and pushed to get a better look at the mysterious beauty who had captivated the prince.

The queen was thrilled. "Who is she?" she demanded.

The king sighed. "What difference does it make?" he said. "They've met, and not a moment too soon."

The queen remembered the bargain they had made with the prince and smiled. "Perhaps that ship won't be setting sail tomorrow after all. You see, darling, I told you this ball would be a good idea."

The king smiled benevolently at his wife. "As always, my dear," he agreed.

Meanwhile, the stepmother and her clumsy daughters were caught up in the curiosity that was sweeping through the ballroom.

"Where did she come from?" Minerva sniffed.

"Look how he's looking at her!" cried Calliope.

"There's certainly something familiar about her," the stepmother said, moving in for a closer look.

A palace guard blocked her view as the prince led Cinderella away from the light and noise of the ballroom and out to the garden.

The prince could not take his eyes off the enchanting young woman in his arms. "Have we met before?" he asked her at last.

Cinderella looked down, not wanting to give away her secret. "I'm sure I would have remembered," she said.

The prince persisted. "I've had the strangest feeling since I first saw you . . . as if I've known you all my life. Do you feel that way, too?"

Cinderella looked into his eyes. "I'm not sure what I'm feeling," she said. "I only know that this has been a magical night, and I don't ever want it to end!"

And as the hands of the clocktower moved closer to midnight, Cinderella and the prince danced by the light of the moon. They had fallen in love.

Chapter 8

It was pandemonium inside the castle. Everyone was anxious to know about the young woman who had stolen the prince's heart, but no one seemed to know anything about her.

"What's so special about *her*?" pouted Calliope.

"What's wrong with us?" whined Minerva.

Their mother was determined to find out. There was something suspicious about the girl, and she was not going to let some nobody come from out of the blue and rob her daughters of a chance to marry the prince! Cinderella did her best to avoid meeting her stepmother's angry gaze, afraid of what might happen should she be recognized.

The king and queen could contain themselves no longer. They rushed onto the dance floor and broke in on the young lovers.

"My son seems to be quite smitten with

you," the king said to Cinderella as he whisked her away from the startled prince.

"I'm lucky to have had a chance to dance with him," Cinderella said shyly.

"I have a feeling he's the lucky one," the king said kindly.

The prince tried to cut in, but to his surprise the queen hurried over and bustled Cinderella away.

"You're very charming, my dear," the queen said to Cinderella. "Do we know your mother and father?"

"I don't think so," Cinderella said in confusion, anxious to return to the prince's side.

He rescued her from more questions. "Mother, the prince would like to have this dance," he said sternly as he took Cinderella's arm and pulled her away.

"I'm sorry about my parents," he apologized.

Cinderella shook her head. "They were lovely," she told him. Then she saw the clock. Alarmed by the time, she said, "I'm sorry, but I have to go now."

The prince frowned. "Why?" he asked.

"I promised someone I would leave by midnight," Cinderella started to say, then she stopped. How could she ever explain?

The prince stepped back, hurt. "It's all right," he said. "Nice meeting you."

Cinderella could see that he didn't understand. "It's not what you think," she tried to say, but the prince stopped her.

"No harm done," he said. "If you'll excuse me, I have one hundred forty-three women waiting for me to dance with them."

"But I thought . . . ," Cinderella said.

"What?' asked the prince, pausing.

"Nothing. I . . . I've got to go," Cinderella said, rushing out of the ballroom before the tears could spill from her eyes.

On the terrace, Cinderella wiped her eyes. It had been such a magical evening. How could it end like this?

"It's not midnight yet," said a familiar voice.

Cinderella looked up to see her fairy godmother standing beside her.

"It doesn't matter. I want to go now," Cinderella said.

"Oh, so you're giving up," her fairy godmother pressed.

"He gave up on me!" Cinderella burst out. "I'm nothing special to him! I'm just one less girl he has to dance with now!"

The fairy godmother shook her head in

dismay. Then she lifted Cinderella's chin and looked her squarely in the eye.

"Cinderella," she said firmly, "you have seven minutes to go back in there and turn this thing around. Now you go march yourself right back in there and get your man! You want all my hard work to be wasted?"

Cinderella blinked back her tears. Her fairy godmother was right. "I hope I make it in time," she thought as she raced back to the ballroom.

As she reached the entrance to the ballroom, there stood the prince, as if waiting for her.

"I'm sorry," he said. "It's just that I don't want you to leave . . . ever. Please stay."

Cinderella spoke quickly, "It's just that I promised my godmother," she said with a sob in her voice.

The prince took her hand and held it to his heart. "I want to meet her," he said. "Your whole family."

Cinderella smiled ruefully. "They may be my family, but they don't really know me. I don't really have anyone at home who listens to me."

The prince nodded solemnly. "I know. I have too many people to talk to, but no one who really can listen. Until you."

For a moment, they just looked into each

other's eyes. Cinderella forgot about the time as the prince spoke.

"Is it possible to meet someone for the first time and know right away that you want to spend the rest of your life with her?" he asked earnestly.

The prince went on. "Is this a dream? I don't ever want to wake up!"

Cinderella could scarcely breathe. "I believe dreams can come true," she said. "It's possible."

The prince leaned forward and pulled her to him in a gentle embrace. As they kissed, the clock began to strike the midnight hour.

Suddenly, Cinderella pulled away. "Midnight!" she cried. "I have to go!"

The prince reached for her but she was already dashing down the steps. "Wait, come back!" he shouted. "I don't even know your name!"

Cinderella ran on, across the terrace and through the great hall.

BONG! BONG! BONG! went the clock.

The prince raced after her, but the throng of guests slowed him down.

"Let me through!" he shouted, pushing to follow Cinderella.

Cinderella lifted her long skirt and flew down

the palace steps. She could hear the prince's voice calling her, but the sound of the clock was more insistent.

BONG! BONG! BONG!

Lionel spotted the prince and hurried over. "Your Highness," he began.

"Out of my way!" cried the prince.

The king and queen rushed over to congratulate their son, only to be shoved aside rudely.

"Come back!" the prince cried. But more and more people got in his way.

"Your Highness, if you would only spend a few more moments with my daughters, I'm sure you would see that they are . . . ," the stepmother said, latching onto the prince's arm.

The prince pushed past her, his eyes blazing. He couldn't let the woman of his dreams vanish into the night!

The clock had almost finished striking twelve. Cinderella reached the carriage. Her hair tumbled around her shoulders, and she was out of breath as she reached for the door.

BONG!

It was midnight. In an instant, the carriage was transformed into a pumpkin once again. Gone were the proud horses. In their place were frightened mice and rats, scurrying for cover.

"Oh, no, oh no!" Cinderella gasped. Her beautiful gown had disappeared, too. Once again she was dressed in rags.

Cinderella could hear the frantic calls of the prince coming closer. In a panic she took off on foot, ignoring the pain of stones and sticks as she ran barefoot over the rocky path. Tears streamed down her cheeks as she ran deeper into the countryside. The farther she ran, the farther away the palace became, until its bright lights were gone and all around her was the cold, dark night.

At the palace, the prince was distraught. The woman of his dreams was gone, and he had no way to find her. Heartbroken, he sat down on the palace steps.

Something on the steps caught his eye. It glittered in the moonlight, beckoning him to pick it up. The prince reached down. It was a tiny slipper, more delicate than anything he had ever seen before. Although it was crystal, there was not a scratch or crack on it. Only one person in the world could have worn such a shoe without breaking it.

The prince clutched the slipper to his chest, and hope began to light up his face.

"It wasn't just a dream," he said to himself. "She was real. I'm going to find her, too." He

looked at the slipper that fit in the palm of his hand and repeated what Cinderella had said to him just a minute before.

"It's possible."

Chapter 9

Cinderella ran through the town, almost blinded by her tears. By the time she reached her home, her stepmother and stepsisters were close behind. Quickly she rushed to her place beside the fire and picked up her sewing.

"What a night!" exclaimed the stepmother as she swept into the room.

"What a magnificent affair!"

Minerva and Calliope agreed. "The most wonderful ball we've ever been to!" they said.

Cinderella looked up innocently. "Did any of you get to dance with the prince?" she asked.

Minerva smirked. "*I* danced about an hour with him!" she declared.

"An hour?" asked Calliope. "Well, then, if you did, I did, too! And he was funnier than I ever imagined."

"Not with me," Minerva said dreamily. "He was so romantic! A poet, really. We were made for each other!"

Cinderella looked down at her sewing to hide her smile. "It sounds like a perfect evening. Did you know everyone at the ball?"

Her stepmother sniffed. "Everyone who's anyone," she said dismissively. "Except for some Princess Something-or-Other. She left early. I suppose she knew she didn't stand a chance with the prince once she saw my daughters there!"

"A princess?" Cinderella asked in surprise. "Did she dance with the prince?"

The stepmother waved the question aside. "He may have."

"She was a little on the cheap side, if you know what I mean," Calliope answered.

"Oh," Cinderella said, trying to conceal her amusement.

"And what have you been up to all evening?" her stepmother asked.

Cinderella smiled. "Oh, dreaming mostly," she answered. "I was dreaming about what it would be like to dance with the prince."

Minerva and Calliope whooped with laughter. "You couldn't possibly dream what *that* is like," they said scornfully.

Cinderella nodded agreeably. "I suppose you're right," she said. "But my dream seemed so real. . . . I think I could even describe what it was like to be there!

"When you waltz with the prince, you whirl around so that your feet don't seem to touch the floor!" Cinderella said.

"That's right!" cried Calliope.

"And it makes you feel like you weigh nothing at all!" Cinderella cried, getting up to twirl around in her bare feet.

"That's right!" exclaimed Minerva.

"How would you know?" the stepmother asked suspiciously.

Minerva and Calliope were caught up in Cinderella's description of the evening, but their mother would hear none of it.

"That's enough!" she shouted suddenly. "Worst nonsense I ever heard! Rubbish and drivel!"

"But Mother!" Calliope cried. The spell was broken.

"Look at the two of you, hanging on her every word! Enough! Go to your rooms! It's late!" shouted the stepmother angrily.

Calliope and Minerva stopped in their tracks, surprised by the sudden rage in their mother's

voice. They started to protest but changed their minds and headed for the stairs.

"Poor Cinderella," said Minerva.

"Imagine her dreaming about what the ball was like," Calliope said.

"It wasn't anything like that," Minerva said with a shake of her head. "Nothing at all."

The stepmother whirled around to assault Cinderella. "And you!" she shouted. "You get your head out of the clouds! Imagine! You dancing with the prince! It's preposterous! Ridiculous!"

Cinderella felt anger growing inside her. Years of listening to her stepmother's abuse came flowing back to her, and at last she could take it no more.

"Why?" she demanded. "Why is that so hard to imagine?"

Her stepmother smiled a wicked smile, delighted for another opportunity to hurt Cinderella. "Well, since you asked," she began sweetly, her voice turning bitter as she spat out the words, "You're common, that's why! Your mother was common, and so are you!"

Cinderella gasped. Never had her stepmother stooped so low as to attack her in this way!

Her stepmother raged on. "Oh, you can wash

your face and put on a clean dress, but underneath you're still common, and no prince would ever have you for your bride."

Cinderella tried to defend herself. "My father . . . ," she began.

But the stepmother was wound up. "Your father was weak! He spoiled you rotten! It's his fault your head is filled with silly dreams that will never come true! Now you listen to me. You will forget about dancing and princes and dreams coming true, because it's impossible! Now clean this place up! It looks like a pigsty!"

With a violent sweep of her cape, the wicked step-mother bolted up the stairs, leaving Cinderella in shock.

Cinderella stood there, numb from the tirade. For a while that evening she had allowed herself to believe her dream really had come true. But the stepmother's words had stung her, and the harsh reality of who she was came crashing down around her.

Cinderella choked back a sob as she reached for her battered suitcase. Like a person in a dream, she slowly put out the fire and began to gather her small, worthless possessions.

Her stepmother's words, loud and coarse, had wiped away all the joy of the evening. Cinderella

had known that the wonderful night would eventually end, but this was more than she could bear.

"Oh, Father, I don't know what to do," she said aloud, tears rolling down her cheeks. "I know I promised I would never leave here, but after tonight I don't see how I can stay.

"Somebody loves me. Oh, I know I can never really marry the prince. But what I've learned is more important. I deserve to be loved, and I really can just go. There's nothing holding me back from going after my dreams, impossible though they may be."

Cinderella closed her eyes as details of the evening came flooding back to her. The magical carriage ride, the brilliance of the palace at night, the beat of the music, her stunning gown, and the handsome prince all became real to her once more.

"All my life, I'll remember this lovely, lovely night," Cinderella said softly to herself. "No one can ever take that away from me."

"Cinderella," a gentle voice said.

Cinderella spun around. There stood her fairy godmother, a look of deep concern on her face.

"If you really love him, why don't you let him know?" she asked gently.

Cinderella shook her head. "The prince?

How can I? Look at me. . . ." She held out the corners of her dirty apron to show the fairy godmother.

Her fairy godmother took her hands in her own. "Do you really think the prince fell in love with you because of your fancy gown or your pretty little beads?" she asked incredulously.

Cinderella pulled away. "I don't know," she answered. "But if you hadn't helped me . . ."

Her fairy godmother interrupted her. "You didn't need my help, honey," she said. "You just thought you did. Don't you trust him to love you as you really are? You're still the same girl he danced with this evening . . . the one he can't get out of his mind."

Cinderella studied her fairy godmother's face, wanting so much to believe what she said.

"Is it still . . . possible?" she asked in a trembling voice. After all that had happened that evening, Cinderella was filled with doubts.

Her fairy godmother held out her arms and wrapped Cinderella in a long, reassuring hug.

Chapter 10

As morning dawned on the palace, the prince was still clutching the tiny glass slipper in his hand, afraid to let it out of his sight.

"She was real!" he told himself over and over. "I must find her!"

The king and queen looked up from their breakfast, not sure how to console their son.

"Sweetheart, you've been up all night," the queen tried. "Please have something to eat. You have to keep your strength up."

The prince shook his head. "I can't," he said gruffly. "I can't eat or sleep until I've found her. She's the one. And this slipper is going to lead me to her."

The king glanced at his wife. "Son," he said gently, "that slipper could belong to any of the young ladies who were at the party last night."

"It's hers!" the prince cried, his voice full of emotion.

The queen motioned to her husband to let her handle things.

"But darling, what do you know about her except that she's beautiful? There were dozens of beautiful young women there last night who didn't go running off like frightened mice. . . ."

The prince stared at his mother as if seeing her for the first time. "You don't get it, do you?" he said. "I love her. She understands me. She knows who I am. Don't talk to me about other young women. She's the one I want. And I tell you, I intend to find her!"

The king listened. He had never heard his son's voice so filled with passion. "Then you must find her," he said, putting his arm around the prince. "When you have found the woman you want to share your life with, it's a miraculous thing. You must find her and never let her go!"

The prince looked gratefully at his father. Perhaps someone else did understand him after all. For the first time in his life, he realized just how deeply his mother and father cared for him and how much they wanted him to be happy.

"We will send out a proclamation," the king told him. "The prince will marry the young lady

who lost this glass slipper. Perhaps someone in the village will know her, and soon we will be planning your wedding celebration!"

At the mention of a wedding, the queen's eyes filled with tears and she jumped up to hug her husband and her son.

As the king and queen left, Lionel rushed in to speak with the prince. The prince greeted him anxiously.

"Any news?" he asked his loyal footman hope-fully. "Does anyone know who she is?"

Lionel was unprepared for the look of dismay on the prince's face when he told him the sorry answer. "No one knows who she is, Your Highness," he said.

The prince turned away. "I don't want to hear it, Lionel!" he cried. "She's out there somewhere, and I'm going to search every inch of this kingdom until I find her!"

The prince looked down at the glass slipper he held in his hand. Reluctantly he held it out to show Lionel.

Lionel looked at the tiny, shimmering object. "This is solid glass!" he exclaimed. "You're telling me that someone actually danced in this? And it didn't break? That's impossible!"

The prince smiled wanly. "It's possible, Lionel," he said. "It's possible."

Lionel examined the shoe, but he couldn't grasp how it could be for real. "Ouch!" he said under his breath.

The prince stood up straight and squared his shoulders. He had made up his mind about something.

"Lionel, we are going to try this slipper on the foot of every young woman in the kingdom. Every last one! And we are going to keep trying until we find the one whom this slipper fits!"

Lionel gasped at the enormous task the prince was describing. "Your Highness . . . ," he started to say.

The prince went on. "When we find the one whose foot this slipper fits, she's the one I am going to marry. Do you understand?"

Lionel was about to try to argue some sense into the prince when a voice from the doorway stopped him.

"Do as he says, Lionel," the queen commanded, not taking her eyes from the prince.

Lionel hurried out, followed by two palace guards. In all his years working for the royal family, he had never had a job like this before!

As the queen watched, the prince grabbed his

sword and his cloak. He turned to his mother as he passed her in the doorway.

"She's waiting for me, Mother," he said, his voice full of confidence. "I'm going to find her."

The queen listened to his footsteps as he ran down the cobbled hall of the palace.

"I hope you do find her, my darling," she said softly. "I hope you do."

Chapter 11

The prince and Lionel set off at a fast clip in the direction of the village. In his hand, the prince held the sparkling glass slipper.

Lionel glanced at the young man. The prince's handsome face wore a faraway look, and he idly stroked the glass slipper, as if for luck.

"A glass slipper!" Lionel muttered. "Impossible!"

The royal carriage bumped over the rocky country roads, but the prince held fast to his precious object. He was determined that no harm should come to it. It would lead him to his true love.

"Are we near the village yet, Lionel?" the prince called impatiently.

The local villagers pointed and whispered at the sight of the grand carriage rumbling into

town. The prince leaned out the window and scanned the faces of those they passed, hoping against hope that the one he loved would be among them.

Not too far off, Cinderella was hurrying in the opposite direction, her eyes fixed on the castle rising beyond the town. As she dragged her battered suitcase behind her, she kept repeating, "It's possible! It's possible!"

A farmer traveling the same path slowed his horse and leaned over to call to Cinderella. "Do you need a ride, miss?" he asked the young woman. She certainly seemed to be in a hurry.

Cinderella looked up gratefully. "Oh, yes! Thank you!" she cried, tossing her bag onto the cart. "I'm going to the palace to see the prince. You see, he's in love with me and I'm in love with him, and, oh . . . ," she sighed and fell back in the hay, overjoyed at the thought of seeing the prince again.

The farmer took one look at Cinderella's dirty, tattered dress and beat-up old suitcase and let out a low whistle. You meet all kinds in this crazy village, he thought as he gave the reins a tug.

As they passed the shops and houses of the village, Cinderella dreamed about the prince and what she would do when she saw him. She was sure that no words would be needed. She was no longer worried about her clothes or her low status. She knew he loved her for who she was.

So wrapped up in her daydreams was Cinderella that she didn't even notice that the wagon was passing under a small bridge.

And at that very moment, the prince's carriage was rumbling across it.

Chapter 12

Word of the prince's quest spread like wildfire throughout the village. Every unmarried woman in town raced out to meet the prince's royal carriage. Toes wriggled nervously as each woman silently hoped that the slipper would somehow fit her own foot.

Lionel and the prince went in and out of every farmhouse, tavern, shop, and inn. The prince wore a determined look on his face as he carried the glass slipper before him. Lionel was less optimistic as he bent over again and again to ease the feet of the village's womenfolk into the delicate slipper.

"Careful, Lionel," the prince warned. An old woman with big, calloused feet was eagerly awaiting her turn. The prince feared that the slipper would break.

Little girls were paraded out by their mothers. Old maids hobbled out of their gardens. Soon a line of women wound through the streets of the town like a snake.

As the sun rose, the day got hotter. With Cinderella beside him, the farmer stopped his hay wagon at the edge of town.

"Something funny is going on here," the farmer said, taking off his cap and scratching his head. "I don't think I'm going to be able to get through."

Cinderella glanced out at the street to see hundreds of women standing barefoot in the street. On any other day she might have been curious as to what the fuss was all about, but today her mind was on one thing only. She had to get to the palace to see the prince.

Cinderella hopped down from the wagon and went over to the well in the center of the village square. As she leaned forward to have a cool drink, the prince's carriage clattered past.

She never saw it, and the prince never saw her. They each continued on their separate ways.

Cinderella pressed on toward the palace. In the daylight it looked even bigger and more forbidding than it had the night before. Cinderella stopped to take a deep breath before going up to a

door in the castle wall. She had no doubts about what she was going to do.

"State your business," a rough voice said through a crack in the door.

Cinderella summoned her courage. "I'm here to see the prince," she said, hoping her voice didn't sound too shaky.

The door opened a bit wider and an unkempt scullery maid peered out at Cinderella. "Speak up!" she demanded.

"I've come to see the prince," Cinderella said, standing up straight.

"You and everybody else," the maid snorted.

Cinderella realized that this wasn't going to be easy.

"You don't understand," she began. "I'm the one he danced with at the ball last night. We . . . we fell in love. I know he'll want to see me."

The scullery maid sized up Cinderella from head to toe. "Oh, sure. You must be the princess who lost the glass slipper!"

Cinderella's face broke into a huge smile of relief. "Yes! Except that I'm not really a princess."

The scullery maid feigned surprise. "You're not? Well, guess what? I'm not really the queen!" And with that she slammed the heavy door in Cinderella's surprised face.

Cinderella stood there, dumbfounded. It had never occurred to her that she might not be allowed to see the prince. But she had come this far and wasn't about to give up all her dreams that easily. Somehow, she was going to find him!

Chapter 13

Back at the stepmother's house, the prince's carriage had just rolled to a creaky stop.

Calliope and Minerva burst into the room as Lionel and the prince entered.

"That's my slipper!" squealed Calliope. "I'd know it anywhere!"

The prince groaned at the memory of dancing with these two the evening before. He fervently wished he had made an exception to his decree of trying the slipper on *every* maiden's foot. But it was too late now, and he would just have to get it over with as quickly as possible.

Calliope extended her big foot in Lionel's direction. Lionel and the prince exchanged weary glances. It was obvious the slipper was not going to fit. Lionel dutifully knelt down with the slipper in hand.

"It's a perfect fit!" Calliope cried as her foot bulged over the top of the delicate shoe.

"Really, miss," Lionel said dryly. He didn't have to say anything more, for Minerva had shoved her sister off the seat.

"Give it to me!" Minerva screeched. "Anyone can see it doesn't fit you! It was made for someone dainty—like me!"

She tried to force her foot into the slipper, but it was no use.

"What have you done to my beautiful slipper?" she cried unconvincingly. "You shrunk it!"

Lionel grabbed the slipper away from her big foot.

The stepmother twisted her hands anxiously, not wanting to let another chance at the prince slip through her fingers. As she glanced out the window, she saw Cinderella coming home with her suitcase. An unbelievable thought occurred to her as she watched Cinderella sneak into the house. Without a word, she slunk over to the cellar door that led to Cinderella's room.

"Is it my fault my feet swell up in this heat?" Minerva wailed. She was determined to have another chance to try on the slipper.

The stepmother reached the door and quickly

locked it. Then with an evil smile she returned to the scene in the hallway.

Cinderella looked up, startled by the click in the door lock.

"Stepmother?" she called, a sense of dread in her heart.

Upstairs, Lionel and the prince were doing their best to beat a hasty retreat.

"Are there any more women in the household?" Lionel asked wearily, hoping desperately that there were not.

"Why, yes," said the stepmother, settling on a low ottoman and lifting her skirt to reveal her foot. "There is one more. . . ."

She reached over and plucked the slipper out of Lionel's hands.

Lionel grabbed the slipper back. "I meant any more young women, Madam!" he implored.

The stepmother frowned at the insult. "How young?" she asked with a threatening edge in her voice.

"Younger than you!" Lionel said, losing his patience.

The stepmother lunged for the slipper and pulled it out of Lionel's grasp. To the astonishment of all, she crammed her large foot into the delicate shoe and held her leg out for all to see.

"It fits!" she cried, unable to believe her own eyes. "Do you see? It fits! It fits! It fits!" And she began to laugh hysterically.

Minerva and Calliope stared open-mouthed at the sight of their mother's huge foot jammed into the tiny slipper. The stepmother's crazy laughter quickly turned to yelps of pain as she screamed.

"It's cutting off my circulation! Get it off! Get it off!" she wheezed, collapsing on the ottoman once more.

Lionel knelt down in an instant to remove the glass slipper, but it wouldn't budge from the swollen foot.

"Get it off!" shrieked the stepmother, pounding his head with her fists. "You imbecile! It's killing me!"

Lionel looked up. "There's no need for name-calling," he said.

Minerva and Calliope joined him in trying to pull the glass slipper off their mother's foot. The prince stood watching in horror as the three of them tugged at the fragile glass slipper.

"Be careful!" he cried, terrified that the slipper would crack. "For heaven's sake, don't damage the slipper!"

"Damage the slipper?" shouted the stepmother

in agony. "What about the damage it's doing to my foot?"

Downstairs, Cinderella was oblivious to the commotion that was going on. She had written a farewell note to her stepmother and gently placed it on the mantel.

"Even if I never find my prince," she whispered, "I know now that the only way for my dreams to come true is to make them happen myself. And so that's why I'm going."

The stepmother was sweating bullets by now, screaming at the top of her lungs.

"One, two, three," said Lionel to Calliope and Minerva. And with a mighty effort they yanked on the shoe, toppling backwards on top of each other as the slipper finally came off.

"What's the matter with you people?" the stepmother cried, rubbing her foot furiously. "Any fool could see that that slipper would never fit me! Oh, I wonder if I'll ever dance again?!" she wailed.

Lionel mopped his brow, grateful to be finished at last with the impossible woman before him.

"Let's go, Your Highness," he said eagerly.

But something had caught the prince's eye. "Not so fast, Lionel," he said thoughtfully.

Chapter 14

"That door, where does it lead?" the prince demanded of the stepmother.

The stepmother glanced uneasily at the cellar door. "Why, only the cellar, Your Highness," she replied sweetly.

The prince stared long and hard at the door. "Are there any other young women in the household?" he asked.

Minerva let out a squeak. Her mother flashed her a warning look.

"No one, Your Highness."

"Not even a servant girl," Calliope piped up helpfully.

The stepmother's eyes flew wide open and her mouth formed a thin, grim line. "That's right, my dear," she said icily.

"Not even a servant girl?" the prince repeated. Something was up.

"I'd like to see your cellar," the prince said suddenly.

"The cellar?" the stepmother asked in amazement. "Oh, Your Highness, it's only a cellar . . . you know, dusty, dark, bugs, the occasional mouse or two. There's nothing to interest you down *there*!"

"I'd like to see for myself, please," the prince insisted. "If you will kindly let me pass. . . ."

At that moment, the stepmother spied the glass slipper, forgotten on its velvet cushion. In a flash, she grabbed it.

"Minerva, quick!" she cried, tossing her prize to her daughter.

Minerva dove for the slipper as it hurtled through the air. Lionel leapt to intercept it, but amazingly, Minerva caught it.

"Over here!" yelled Calliope.

The confused Minerva threw it to her sister, who jumped to catch it.

"Ladies, please!" cried Lionel as he darted back and forth across the room trying to retrieve the slipper.

As the sisters volleyed the glass slipper across the room, their mother took hold of the prince's sleeve.

"Take one of my daughters for your bride,

Your Highness. Please! They really are more clever than they look! All right, they may be a little rough around the edges, but in all the kingdom you'd be hard-pressed to find girls as talented and . . . ," she begged hopelessly.

The prince cut her off. "Madam, I command that you stop this foolishness this instant!"

The stepmother let out a defeated sigh. She reached a forlorn hand out to take the glass slipper from Minerva—and to everyone's utter shock, she threw it with all her might out the window!

"Oops!" she said wickedly.

The prince raced out the door, his heart pounding. To his amazement, the slipper had landed on a soft bed of moss. There wasn't a scratch on it.

He knelt to lift it with trembling hands. Suddenly, he noticed something else there on the soft grass.

Two tiny bare feet were standing beside him. The prince looked up. There stood Cinderella, her suitcase in her hand.

He gasped, unable to take his eyes off her. Cinderella felt a lump in her throat as their eyes met.

"You ever feel like you want to run away somewhere and never come back?" the prince

asked her softly.

Cinderella nodded.

"Pardon me, what did you say your name was?" the prince asked as he moved slowly toward her.

"Cinderella," she said, her voice a whisper.

The prince smiled. He had found her at last!

"I like it. Cinderella," he said.

"It grows on you, I guess," she said softly.

The prince held out the glass slipper. "May I?" he asked her.

Cinderella nodded as the prince knelt down with the glass slipper. She held out her tiny foot and smiled as the prince started to slip the shoe on.

"No!" shrieked the stepmother,

"Quiet, woman!" ordered Lionel.

They all watched in astonishment as the prince gently fitted the slipper onto Cinderella's outstretched foot. The slipper began to sparkle and shimmer magically as it slid firmly on.

Suddenly, the fairy godmother appeared. She waved her wand over Cinderella, and a shower of sparkling stars flew around her.

Minerva and Calliope screamed and covered their faces.

Cinderella's ragged dress was transformed

once again into the beautiful ball gown of the evening before. Her hair swept up magically into a glossy pile of curls. Her face glowed with a smile of joy.

Feeling faint, the stepmother grabbed the doorpost.

"Cinderella?" she gasped.

The prince lifted Cinderella's chin and leaned forward to kiss her tenderly.

"It's possible!" sang the fairy godmother as the young lovers kissed. "Impossible things happen every day!"

And as they set off for the kingdom to live happily ever after, Cinderella knew that her dreams really had come true.